I0684166

Voices From the Gray

Voices From the Gray

13 Tales of Ghosts, Demons, and the Unknown Vol.1

Elizabeth Casanova

To my family and friends who believe in me

Copyrights

Voices From the Gray: 13 Tales of Ghost, Demons, and the Unknown Vol.1
Copyright © 2021, Elizabeth Casanova
Self-published
Designed by Elizabeth Casanova
elizabeth.casanova.author@gmail.com

All rights reserved.
No part of this publication may be reproduced, stored in a retrieval system,
stored in a database, and/or published in any form or by any means, electronic,
mechanical, photocopying, recording, or otherwise, without the prior written
permission of the publisher.

Contents

Preface

I'm writing this book in hope to give light to those who also see things from the unknown. With a better understanding of our energies, we could acknowledge the difference between light and dark spirits. Some only want to be heard or seen while others intended to cause harm. We must not fear these entities for the living are more terrifying.

I would like to thank my family and friends for giving me the strength to become a writer. I would have never found the confidence to complete this book without them. I also give thanks to my readers, whom I hope will enjoy these eerie stories.

Introduction

This book is based on my real experiences with the unknown or supernatural. From the first story to the last, I show the different entities I've encountered while growing up. I also give insight by showing my interactions with the light and dark spirits. Though most of them terrified me, I tried my best to understand what they wanted to say.

- 1 -

The Three Children

It all began when I was seven years old. I had fallen very ill and had to stay overnight at the hospital. The nurses were quite surprised at how quiet I was during the various tests and x-rays I had to go through without making a fuss. The loud machinery and needles didn't scare me. If anything, I was curious about how the machines worked or how they were made. I still remember the nurses patting my head as they passed by and telling me how "sweet and quiet" I was when they saw me. Some even doubled back just to talk to me again.

My aunt dropped off some books and blankets for me and my mom to keep our minds busy for the remainder of the night. This was before Iphones and tablets existed. During the night, nurses would come into the room to check my vitals, speak to my mom softly, and leave as quietly as they came. It was only my mom and I in the hospital room. I could hear the rhythmic beep of the heart monitor and the sound of footsteps from the nurses walking down the halls. The light above my bed only lit up our side of the room leaving the empty hospital bed beside us in the dark. My eyes began to close and soon enough I fell asleep.

I suddenly woke up to the sound of children laughing. The curtain that divides the room was pulled forward, covering my view. I turned to my mom but she was sleeping in the chair next to me. I could tell the light was off from the other side by seeing the darkness below the curtain and I wondered if they had moved someone in while we were sleeping. I reached out with my tiny arms as far as I could to pull aside the curtain and see who was there. After I pulled back the curtain, I saw three children staring at me from behind the empty hospital bed.

Though It was dark, I could still manage to see their faces. They all wore hospital gowns and had large dark eyes with massive smiles that ran from one side of their face to the other. I waved to them saying hello but they were startled by my quick movements. I thought it was weird but I still wanted to figure out who they were or why they were in the room. I told them that they could come over and step into the light so I could see them more clearly. They whispered to each other for a brief moment before walking over to my bed. When they were walking towards me, their shadows merged into a large dark mass behind them. An uneasy and strange feeling came over me.

They were standing at the edge of where the light above my bed began, almost as if they did not want to be touched by it. Though they were still in the dark, they were close enough for me to see their individualistic features. The shortest one had short thin hair with a smile that seemed larger than the rest of his face. His hospital gown dragged along the floor making the material on the edges dirty and wrinkled. The tallest one was very thin to the point where I could see her cheek and collar bones. Her thin arm wrapped around the other child like a vine around a tree. The third one had bandages on one side of her face and arm. She was the only one who seemed to have trouble walking on her own.

I told them, "It's ok, you can come closer. Nothing will happen." They all looked at each other with their big dark eyes and whispered low enough for me not to hear what they were saying. At this point, I was more curious than frightened about the situation. Again, I reached out my arm signaling them to come over, reassuring them that nothing will happen if they do. They all turned their heads at me and began to step forward into the light.

A voice broke out of the silence. "What are you doing?" My mom had a confused expression on her face as she asked me that question. I turned over to point at the children in the room but they were gone as if they vanished into thin air.

I told my mom about the children in the room and pointed towards the spot I last saw them. She got up and looked around the room turning on the main light to see if anyone else was there with us. She even checked the closet shelf and restroom but there was no sign of anyone around. The night was just as quiet as before. My mom sat back down on her chair and told me "maybe it was just a dream" and that everything is okay.

My mom and I were talking for a bit since we couldn't go back to sleep then a nurse walked into the room to check on my vitals. I asked the nurse if there were other kids in the hospital that night but she stated that I was the only one on the second floor. She gave me medicine, patted my head, and left the room. I slept soundly for the remainder of the night.

After I was discharged, we went to our house and I was told to rest for the remainder of the day. My sisters were still in school so I had the room to myself for a while. I fell asleep and woke up to the sound of voices. They were faint but it was loud enough to wake me from my sleep. I saw something move in the corner of my eye to where the bedroom door was. I turned in its direction and saw that it was the same three children from the hospital. They were peeking at me outside the bedroom door. This time they seemed different.

The sunlight from my window made the children have this golden aura around them. The smiles on their faces didn't seem creepy and menacing as they did that night at the hospital. Their clothes were bright and colorful instead of dull and dirty. I rubbed my eyes to make sure if I was seeing clearly but they vanished once again. This was the first but not the last time I saw something that I believe to be supernatural.

Grandmother's Bloodline

When my grandparents would visit us down in the valley from west Texas, we would all gather at their ranch and have a big family cookout. Their ranch was quite isolated from the city and was surrounded by tall pine trees that would howl as the wind blew between them. The small pond behind the house made me feel uneasy because the water was always murky and lifeless. In times of drought, it would completely dry up leaving a dead crater in the earth. At night, my grandparent's ranch was surrounded by complete darkness and the only sound around was the chirping of crickets or the howling of the trees.

It was early summer and my grandparents finally came down to visit. We had our traditional family cookout at their ranch. Everyone had different tasks of making food, cleaning, and setting the dining tables out on the front patio. Us children were instructed to stay out of the way and play outside on the swing set or watch tv. I never liked staying in the house because it was always dark no matter how much sunlight was shining in and it gave me an uneasy feeling. The old dark stained wood walls smelled of smoke and moisture. It was suffocating to me. Especially in the summer heat. The windows made everything on the other side look lifeless. Overall, the entire house had always felt ominous to me.

Instead of staying inside, I went to play with my older sister Christina on the swingset. The noise of music and loud voices were hushed by the gentle wind. I began to swing as high as I could but came to a sudden stop when something caught my eye in between the trees across the swingset. It was a shadow slowly moving towards us. I asked Christina to stop swinging and look at it but she brushed me off. It got closer and I was able to see a silhouette of a tall thin person. I grabbed Christina's swing, practically demanding her to stop and look at the shadow figure. When I pointed in its direction, the shadow then leaned behind one of the trees. She gasped and ran inside leaving me behind. I was also frightened but I wanted to know if it was our cousins playing a prank or a person lurking in the trees.

I slowly walked towards the tall pine trees beside the pond. The trees howled, silencing everything behind me completely. I peeked around to see if anyone was there but there was only the maze of trees. When I took a step in, a twig under my feet snapped then I heard a voice yell, "Liz, get over here! Don't play by the pond!" My mom was standing by the swings waiting for me to get back. I ran to the patio in front of the house and played with my cousins who had just arrived.

The food was finally ready and everyone was outside sitting on the tables enjoying each other's company. Like always, the adults sat all together and us kids were all grouped up in our own mini table. The table I was sitting at, pointed towards the pine trees by the pond. I couldn't help but look into them wondering if I was going to see the shadow again. After everyone was done eating, we played Loteria, musical chairs, and played basketball for a while. The sun had set and my grandparents' ranch became submerged in darkness.

We all gathered by the small fire pit my uncles had placed near the swingset. We ate smores while talking for hours. I had the urge to go to the restroom so I headed inside asking my oldest sister Yoli to accompany me. Inside the house was quiet and the only light on was from the poorly lit living room. All the other rooms were in the dark. The open doors looked like portals into the underworld. Yoli was just as creeped out as I was. She told me to hurry up so we could back outside and join the others.

I opened the restroom door and turned on the light to check for spiders and snakes because they occasionally appeared in the house randomly. I didn't notice anything until I looked in the living room before closing the restroom door. I saw a man wearing an old military uniform next to the window and tv. He was holding a rifle between his arm and chest with a blank expression on his face. Yoli was standing in front of the door to hold it open. This blocked her view from the man on the other side.

Yoli is the biggest scaredy-cat in the family so I didn't want to startle her by saying, "A man standing behind the door." The man's military uniform looked like he was from the Mexican-American War period. He was translucent as I could see the old walls and picture frames behind him. I didn't feel afraid but I wanted to leave anyway.

I looked at him while walking out of the house. Yoli followed behind asking me what was going on. I told her I saw a big tarantula and that we should leave. When we got back with the others, I whispered to my mom that I saw a man in the house. My mom looked at me for a moment and told my uncles to see if anyone was lurking in or around the house. They didn't find anyone so we all continued to sit around the firepit.

Everyone was having fun, laughing, and eating snacks until we all heard a crackling sound coming from the darkness within the trees. The adults said it was probably an old branch falling off to keep us "kids" from getting scared. This inspired my family into talking about ghost stories and unexplained things they have experienced growing up. Each one of their stories was thrilling enough to make our skin crawl.

I noticed that most of my family from my grandmother's side were the ones who were experiencing these creepy events as they were growing up. This made me remember the children I saw at the hospital and thought to myself, "maybe it's only us who can see these spirits." The cracking sound happened again, making everyone go silent as it was louder than before. The wind blew faintly and the howl of the trees filled the air. The surrounding darkness seemed endless as we stared into it. We all began to hear laughing in the distance. It sounded like a group of old women cackling but with a raspiness to their voices. Everyone jumped up and began to look all around trying to figure out where the laughter was coming from. It grew louder and louder by the second until it turned into screaming.

Some of my cousins covered their ears because the sound was horrible and terrifying. I stood silently beside my mom and Yoli. We all began to slowly walk towards the house while still looking into the surrounding darkness. My uncles stayed by the fire pit waiting to see if they would find anyone out there. Suddenly Yoli accidentally stepped on our dog's tail, making him yelp loudly. This triggered everyone into running inside the house.

We all giggled at how silly we reacted and luckily our dog's tail was alright. My uncles went to investigate where the laughter came from while us kids stayed inside with our mothers and grandmother. They didn't find anyone but we all took it as a queue to leave the ranch and head out to our houses. My grandparent's house was too small to fit everyone in for the night so only a few stayed behind. Everyone cleaned their mess, folded tables, folded chairs, and packed plates to go. As I was moving the chairs, I saw a shadow in the corner of my eye by the front patio. I ignored it and tried to clean up as quickly as possible so we could leave already. After everyone said their goodbyes and got into our cars, I saw the shadow again. It was leaning beside the garage that is in front of the driveway. As we were driving away, The shadow was peeking at us from the dark beside the garage.

I remember asking my mom that night before going to bed, "why do I see things that others can't see?" She sat beside me and told me about my grandmother's bloodline. My grandmother comes from a long line of people who are sensitive to the energy that surrounds us. Mostly the women in the family have a stronger ability to sense these energies and can see or hear those who are no longer living or part of this living world. Those who don't have these abilities hold healing auras like my grandmother did.

My grandmother held this strong energy that I could never fully explain. She was like a magnet that made random strangers talk to her to get things off their chest. I remember people asking her if she could make a prayer for them and she always did without hesitation. She would place her hand on their shoulder and pray for what they asked for. My grandmother didn't care if other people stared at them, or thought she was crazy. Once the prayer was done, the people would hug her and leave with an added brightness to them. Though I found it strange at times, I always respected my grandmother and her powerful faith.

After learning the history of my grandmother's bloodline, I felt more at ease because it meant I wasn't going crazy or seeing things that aren't there. It was only spirits or beings trying to communicate with me. This created my interest in learning about ghosts, demons, and other entities that lurk on the other side.

- 3 -

The Canopy

I was stuck in summer school and I was playing with my classmates on the school playground. The canopy in the distance had an energy to it that beckoned for my attention. Time after time I'd find myself looking at the pillars under the canopy. I was standing still for a minute, staring, until I heard the coach blow their whistle. Our break was over and we lined up to head back to class.

As we were passing the second and third-grade building, I saw a kid standing in the hallway through the door windows. It looked strange but I thought, "Maybe someone is headed to the restroom." Though it made me feel a bit uneasy, I tried not to ponder on it.

The following day I had the same uneasy feeling about the canopy and no matter how hard I tried, I kept looking in that direction. This went on for about a week until we had a thunderstorm. The thunder rumbled as we stayed inside all morning watching movies and playing board games. When the rain and thunder grew louder everyone suddenly became quiet and looked at each other while trying not to freak out. The teacher paused the television when the wind howled loudly and opened the door to look outside from the hall. We all peeked behind the teacher to see the wind and rain blowing against the glass windows. The blue hue of the clouds seeped in the hall making it appear as if we were underwater. The teacher told us to go sit down at our desk while he talked to his coworker in the hallway.

As I walked back towards my desk, I heard something move in the corner of the classroom so I turned to see what it was. My friend next to me saw my reaction and asked "what is it?" This got the attention of the other students and they all looked at the same spot. The hair on the back of my neck stood up and my arms felt cold. A thunderbolt broke the dead silence and the lights went out. The other kids ended up freaking out and tried to find where the teacher went. I turned back to the corner where the noise came from and saw a little boy standing in the dark. He was pointing to my friend's desk with an expressionless face.

I wanted to know what he was pointing at so I walked over to the desk. My arms felt as if they were freezing. I looked into the cubby and found my friend's sweater tucked inside. It's black wool-like fabric melted in my hands as I picked it up. I couldn't help but think "maybe he wants the sweater?" I began to walk towards the boy with the sweater in my hands. His eyes pierced the darkness as he stood silently in the corner of the room. I heard the sound of water dripping on the floor as I got closer to the boy. My fingers began to feel as if I was holding ice but I was determined to give the boy the sweater. As I was only a few steps away from him, I was able to see more detail on his appearance.

The boy looked like he had been out in the rain. The water from his hair dripped into the puddle under him. He had on a basic t-shirt with a pair of jeans. His clothes had dirt stains scattered on them.

Though he was pointing at the sweater, I could see his other arm pressed against his left side. He was shivering in the dark and his expressionless face made me feel sad. I felt as if he wanted to say he was cold but was refrained from doing so. When he continued to point at the sweater, I saw the discoloration of his fingers. They were a dark blue or purple color followed by a red hue on the end of the knuckle. His eyes still pierced the darkness as I looked upon his face.

I was about to give the boy the sweater when the lights suddenly turned back on. Everyone was staring at me with my arm out holding the sweater. "What are you doing?", a classmate asked me judgingly. I could hear them whispering to each other about how "weird" I was. I placed my friend's sweater back and sat down on my desk.

When it was lunchtime, my friend asked me what I was doing with his sweater. I told him about what I saw and he started to freak out a bit. "You saw a ghost!", he exclaimed blaringly while we were walking in line to the cafeteria. The other kids from class gasped and wanted to know the whole story. I told them after lunch I would tell them in class. When we sat down at the tables in the cafeteria, I felt uneasy again. I looked through the large glass doors and saw the canopy outside. I couldn't see clearly but I was sure someone was standing alone beside the pillars.

My arms began to feel cold. Though I had a sweater of my own, I still felt as if I was standing in the freezing rain. I asked my friend if he could see anyone outside but a classmate overheard and told the others. They all got excited and ran towards the glass doors hoping to see something. The teachers saw the commotion and told us to sit back down. Everyone was in a rush to go back to class because they wanted to hear about what I saw earlier when the lights went out.

We all moved our desks to make space on the floor to sit in a circle. Our teacher didn't seem to care and left to talk to his co-worker next door. It was still raining and the lights would flicker when lightning struck close by. Everyone peered in as I described the boy and told them what I think he wanted. I remember saying, "He looked like he was standing in the rain because he was wet and cold. When he pointed at the sweater, I noticed his fingers were darker than the rest of his hands." My friend shivered, muttering how creepy it was under his breath.

I asked my friend where he got his sweater and he told us he found it at the park near the college campus in town. The kids who believed me stayed. Those who didn't left the group circle to do something else. We all decided to discuss what we should do about the boy or spirit. We talked until it was time to go home. I told my friend to bring his sweater tomorrow and that I would give him an extra one I had as a replacement. He was cool with it and agreed to the offer.

When I got home, my arms felt cold no matter how many blankets I covered myself with. I was hoping I wouldn't see the boy leering around the house in the middle of the night so I tried to fall asleep early. I woke up to use the restroom but heard our dogs barking outside. I went over to look out the front window thinking they were barking at a cat but I was wrong. I saw the boy standing in the middle of the street. This caught me off guard and I ran back to my bed. I could still hear our dogs barking as I hid under the covers.

The following day I brought the sweater and noticed my friend had an extra pair of shoes. He had a tired look on his face when he walked up to me. I asked him why he looked so tired and he replied, "I had a creepy dream about the boy you saw and my shoes fell off in my dream. Maybe he wants shoes too?"

When it was time to play outside, we went to the canopy to leave the items for the boy in the center pillars. The pillars were side by side and there was a small opening in the middle of them. We squeezed the sweater and shoes through the opening which made them kind of hidden. We told the other kids in class not to touch the stuff because they are meant for the spirit. The other kids just snickered at us and went along about their day.

The sweater and shoes stayed in the same spot for about a week but then disappeared. I'm sure a teacher or coach picked up the items and placed them in the lost and found. After that, I never saw that boy or spirit again. We unintentionally started a tradition among the students of leaving treats next to the pillar for the ghost or spirit.

4

Mirror Mirror

One summer weekend my family and I went to the park near the college campus in town. It had recently been renovated and new gazebos were installed for families to sit or gather around in the shade. My sisters and I were riding on our new bikes along the bike trail while my parents were walking at their own pace. My sister Christina wanted to start a race with me so she yelled out, "I bet I'm faster than you!" I took the bait and started to pedal my bike as fast as I could to at least catch up with her. We headed at top speed until I bumped into a rock on the path and fell over. I got up and tried to walk it off.

I told Christina I was going to wash my hands and clean up my knee since it got scraped up from falling. She waited by my bike as I went to the newly installed restrooms from the gazebos. Like any curious kid, I looked around to see the tiles, sinks, and other things that are usually in public restrooms. I washed my hands and put some soap on a napkin to clean my knee. It stung a bit but not as much as I thought it would have. When I was rinsing off the soap, I heard the restroom door open. I looked around to see if anyone was there but it was empty. I decided to continue to clean myself up and walked back to the sink.

The hair behind my neck began to rise and I felt out of breath. Suddenly a loud clicking noise behind me got my attention. I noticed a girl was standing beside me in the reflection of the mirror. I was frozen in shock. She had on a striped shirt and light jeans with a blue and purple jacket. Her hair was long as it clung to both sides of her face. She looked the same age as my oldest sister Yoli, who was a teenager at the time.

I could see the girl mouthing something but I couldn't quite make it out. Her face grew angrier by the moment as I stood still in silence. She dropped her jaw down as if she was going to let out a monstrous scream. Christina, impatient as always, bursted through the restroom door, telling me to hurry up. The girl vanished, leaving me unable to explain why I took long.

Christina dragged me out so we could continue riding our bikes at the park. I tried not to limp but my mom noticed right away and asked me what happened. She ended up getting a few bandaids from her large purse to put over my scrapes and cuts. After patching up, we all sat at a table near the bike trail to eat some sandwiches we had packed earlier.

The sound of wind blowing through the mesquite trees and the feeling of fresh air felt therapeutic from the table under the shade. Families passed by walking or on their bikes and skates as they too enjoyed the new renovations of the park. I was in my own world enjoying my lunch until a boy fell over while skating. As I walked over to him, I saw the same girl from the mirror in the distance. Her mouth was moving but I still couldn't understand what she was saying. When I helped the boy up, his clothes were covered in dirt and his face was red with embarrassment. I told him it was okay because I also fell down and pointed to my bandages to show proof.

When I was talking to the boy, the girl was still in the shadows looking at me. I heard a hiss coming from the tree above us. There was a snake draped on a branch and we both ran, afraid to get bit. I ended back to where my family was sitting down and didn't notice the boy had followed me. He asked my parents if he could wait with us until his mother got to where we were at. The park is about the size of a football stadium so it wouldn't be long till his mother found him. We gave him some snacks and juice while he stayed at our table. I looked back to the tree to see if the girl was still there but she was gone. The boy's mother arrived and thanked us for watching over him till she got there.

We stayed for about another hour until it was time to leave. My sisters and I ended up knocking out as soon as we entered the house. Our mom woke us up and told us to clean up before dinner started. I shared a room with Christina. It had a long thin mirror hanging on the wall across the bedroom closet and our beds were on the opposite sides of the room. After getting out of the bathroom, I saw the girl from the park sitting on the edge of my bed in the reflection of the mirror. I heard Christina gasp as she stopped behind me. She turned away and ran to the kitchen where my mom was.

I slowly opened the door with my hand. I felt my heart racing and the hair behind my neck stood up. The girl was looking towards my backpack. I walked over, still keeping my eyes on her as I opened the zipper. Her lips were moving but no sound was coming out. I grabbed a pencil and paper from my bag and began to write down what I thought she was trying to say. I tried over and over again but she grew angrier with every wrong answer. The girl lunged at me, making me fall back. She disappeared and I stayed in silence on the floor. I tried to make sense of what was happening.

I kept it to myself for the rest of the night and tried to forget it. When it was time to go to bed, I saw the girl again in the mirror.

Her face was peeking out of the closet between the hung jackets and sweaters. Christina was already sleeping in her bed. I said faintly, "I don't understand." The girl moved back, disappearing into the closet. I fell asleep soon after.

A cold voice whispered in my ear, "They will speak." I woke up immediately, looking around in the dark. Christina was covered under her blankets. She has always slept that way for as long as I could remember. I went over to see if she was playing a prank on me but she was asleep. I wrote down what I heard and left the note in my bag. I sat up in my bed until I got tired and fell back to sleep.

We went back to the park a few weeks later. I took the note with her words "They will speak" written down and left it in the restroom where I had first encountered her. I thought maybe she wanted someone to find it and only they would understand the message. This event made me very wary of mirrors. I always feel that if I stare too long into the mirror, I might see her again.

5

Stairs

When I was little, my mom would visit my aunt Betty at her apartment across town. I remember we would watch movies together or I would play with my cousin Noe while our moms talked on the patio.

One day while I was in the living room in Betty's apartment, I saw a shadow pass the kitchen window. I went over to figure out what it was. I noticed the shadow had an odd shape and swung from one side to the other. Through the tiny opening of the curtain, I saw that it was a pair of feet. It looked like someone was hanging. Her apartment didn't have a balcony which added to my confusion because, how else would someone be able to do that?

I was too short to open the curtain so I had to grab an extra chair from the mini closet under the stairs. When I opened the closet door, I saw a man standing behind the foldable iron table my aunt had inside. I gasped out of shock and closed the door. This caught my mom's attention and she asked me what happened. I didn't want to scare Betty since she lived alone with Noe so I told my mom I saw a huge roach crawling in there. My mom opened the door and looked but nothing was there. I even peeked behind her to check for myself.

Noe and I ended up playing in the parking lot until it was time for dinner. We all sat in the living room eating around the short table on the floor. I sat facing towards the kitchen. There was still enough light from the sun to glow through the curtain. My mom asked me to place the dishes in the sink since we were done eating. As I was placing the plates down in the sink, I saw the shadow in the window again. The silhouette swung in the same pattern as before. Left. Right. Left. Right. I reached over with a spatula in my hand to open the curtain but Noe called me over to the living room so the four of us could watch a movie together.

We ended up watching old classical movies until the sun had set. Since it was late, Betty asked my mom to stay the night since she didn't want to be alone. She had a two-story apartment. The bedroom and bathroom were upstairs while the kitchen and living room were on the first floor. She set up a mattress for us all to bunk down in the living room together. We were not tired yet so we decided to play some board games throughout the night. Betty and Noe are used to sleeping in complete darkness. I remembered the man I saw earlier in her apartment and dreaded the moment when they would turn off all the lights.

It was time to sleep and all the lights were off except the bathroom light up the stairs. Luckily the lights from the street were able to shine through the apartment, preventing total darkness downstairs. Before I laid down, I noticed the closet door was open. I asked who opened it but my mom and Betty dismissed my question and told me to go to sleep. I walked over and closed the door myself before lying down.

I remember having a strange dream that night that I will never forget. In my dream, I was walking down the road at night where Betty lived. Back then there were no supermarkets or stores nearby so the road was very quiet and secluded. It was the same in my dream. While I was walking, my footsteps got louder and louder and my breathing began to pace up. I looked into the trees next to the road and saw the figure of a man standing there in the dark. When I stopped walking, the street light above me began to flicker. I tried to run but something was holding me back. I looked down at my ankle and saw the man holding my foot down while he was on the floor. His clothes looked dirty and his face and skin were rotten. I suddenly woke up to the sound of a door opening.

I turned over and saw the closet door open. Everyone was asleep so I went over to close it by myself. Nothing happened. I felt the urge to use the restroom and began to walk up the stairs. When I was halfway up the stairs, I saw a tall slender shadow figure standing on the top step. My breath became heavy and I felt as if I was about to pass out. I couldn't move or speak no matter how hard I tried. It felt like an eternity just standing there looking at it. What freaked me out was that the shadow looked like it had hooved feet and horns. I thought, "This can't be real" and tried to go back downstairs. Slowly but surely, I was able to move my feet and go back to the living room. I was so frightened that I hid under the covers without telling anyone.

The silence was so loud that I felt as if my ears would pop. My heart was beating crazy so I began to breathe slowly and calm myself down. I peeked out of the covers to see if it had followed me but I saw nothing. The orange streetlights and the buzzing of the electricity were my only company as I lied awake. I began to count in my head until I fell asleep.

The next day, I woke up and felt some pressure on my ankle. When I rolled my sock down, I saw a small bruise in the shape of a thumbprint. I told my mom about what I saw and my weird dream that night. She told Betty and they both ended up blessing the apartment with some holy water. I thought to myself that everything would turn out ok and hopefully I would never see that figure and shadow again.

When we left Betty's apartment, I felt as if a huge weight got lifted from my body.

A few days later, Betty called my mom and told her that one of the apartment complexes where she lived had caught on fire. Thankfully no one was hurt as the fire had only stayed in the kitchen. Hearing that brought shivers to my spine and made me wonder, what if I saw a bad omen the night my mother and I stayed.

6

Orange Light

Once again, I found myself at Betty's apartment with my mom. She asked me to keep her company because my other sisters wanted to stay home. Though I was still afraid of what I saw last time, I didn't want to leave my mom alone.

I was outside playing in the parking lot with Noe as our moms sat on the sidewalk to keep an eye on us. As I was standing in the parking lot waiting for Noe to throw the ball, I heard a coin fall behind me. I turned around to see if anything fell out of my pocket but nothing was there. A bird flew past me, making me move out of its way. Noe laughed for a moment and said we should take a small break. We walked over to our moms and asked them if we could get juice from the fridge. They said yes and we ran inside trying to see who was the fastest.

Noe won the race and opened the fridge to get the last kool-aid pouch. I reached over to the sink to grab a glass of water. When I reached over to open the faucet, I saw a severed hand in the drain. I jumped back in shock dropping the glass cup on the floor. Noe looked into the sink and yelled, "what is it?" Our moms heard the commotion and ran inside. I told them I saw a spider climbing up the drain and that I thought it was going to jump at me. They inspected the drain and found nothing. Once the glass was cleaned up, we all sat down on the sidewalk to enjoy the sunny day until dinner.

Noe and I were watching T.V while our moms were cooking. I walked to the kitchen to grab plates and utensils to set up the table in the living room. In the corner of my eye, I saw a shadow in the kitchen window. I looked at my mom and Betty but they didn't notice it. The shadow was swinging just like before. Moving left to right rhythmically.

Fear filled my chest. I couldn't move and the only thing I was able to do was to look at it. After a moment of stillness, a bird slammed onto the kitchen window. Luckily the glass didn't break and the bird was gone. I guess I was the only one who heard it because my family didn't react to the noise. I finished setting up the table and tried not to pay too much attention to the spirits because it might get worse if I do.

After dinner, we went outside to play and everything seemed fine. The other kids who lived in the apartments were also out in the parking lot. Our mothers were huddled together talking and laughing while keeping an eye on us. The sun was setting and people began to go inside or leave the apartment complex.

Our mothers called us to go inside. Noe had thrown the ball and it rolled under a car across the parking lot. I went over to get it and as I did, I saw a pair of men's shoes on the other side of the car. I jumped up, stepping away from the car and getting a good distance. Noe ran over telling me what's wrong. Again, no one was there. I told him I couldn't reach under the car to grab the ball so he got it instead.

We began to walk towards the apartments. Our moms greeted us on the sidewalk and we all began to go inside. In the corner of my eye, I saw a man standing on the far edge of Betty's apartment. Thinking it could be a creep, I told my mom right away. She had a concerned face and went to look with Betty outside. They didn't find anyone and informed the security guard that patrols the apartments just in case someone was actually out there.

We continued our normal routine and played board games for a bit while we talked about random things. I had to go to the restroom so I began to walk towards the stairs. When I was on the first step, I remembered the shadow and stopped for a moment. I thought about asking my mom to go with me up the stairs but I didn't want to seem like a baby. I decided to go alone. I could hear my family laughing and playing games downstairs from the second floor.

When I was done using the restroom, I saw someone standing on the other side of the door. The shadow of their feet was visible on my side of the door. I stood in silence, hesitant to open the door. I said in a low voice, "Hello?" but no answer. When I turned the doorknob, the shadow moved away. I opened the door to peek out. Betty's bedroom door was slightly open. I wasn't sure if it already was before I used the restroom. I heard something tumble in her room so I walked over. "Hello?" I called out again and the result was the same. Nothing. I pushed open the door and saw that her room was completely dark. I heard the thump again and noticed it came from the window. I walked a bit further into the room to find out what was making that sound. My eyes focused on a plastic bag that was caught on the rails of the window. It was brushing against the glass, replicating the tumbling sound I heard.

Suddenly I felt my hair begin to rise on the back of my neck. I turned around slowly and saw a figure of a man standing at the edge of the room. My heart was pounding as if it wanted to burst out of my chest. My feet wanted to freeze as I stared at the man. His face was disfigured and he had on a coat that was way bigger than his actual size. He was slightly swaying back and forth in the dark. His face entered in and out of the hallway light through the open bedroom door. He suddenly began to walk towards me and made a break for it. I made it to the hallway and looked behind to see if the man was following me.

My mom yelled from downstairs, "what's going on up there?" I told her it was nothing and took another look into Betty's room. It was empty but I still felt uneasy as I looked around. I went back downstairs to continue our game. My mom asked Betty if she wanted us to stay since I mentioned seeing a man around her apartment. Betty said yes and we all gathered around in the living room to go to sleep.

I tried to stay calm and composed as we were assembling the mattresses and blankets. Dread filled my mind as I kept thinking, what will I do once they turn off all the lights? I hoped I wouldn't see anything for the rest of the night but I had a feeling I was going to. I avoided drinking water before laying down so I wouldn't have to go to the restroom in the middle of the night. Before we laid down, I told my mom I felt a bit uneasy but she reassured me that everything will be alright. Soon the lights were off and all of us fell asleep.

I woke up to a small bang in the kitchen. I tapped my mom's shoulder to wake her up but she was asleep. A faint scuffling sound appeared in the same direction. The incandescent colors of the streetlight seeped through the kitchen window, making it look like it was illuminated by fire. I stood up silently for a moment while looking through the kitchen doorway. Still hearing the noise in the kitchen, I decided to go over.

I walked silently towards the kitchen clenching both of my fists to try and stay calm. When I got to the kitchen, I saw the man from Betty's room on the kitchen floor. His body was twisted and torn like gum that was pulled and stuck between gears. The blood under him glowed under the orange light that seeped through the kitchen window. The man's hand began to move and reach towards me. He kept gasping for air as if he was drowning in his own blood. Slowly by slowly he began to drag his body closer to me. As he was only a couple of inches away from my feet, he pointed behind me. His eyes met mine for a moment then widened when he looked behind me. He was filled with complete and utter fear. The hair on the back of my neck stood up and my stomach dropped for I knew what it was.

My eyes began to tear up as I forced myself to turn around. I saw the same shadow figure from the top of the stairs. It was standing on the edge of the living room next to my family who was sound asleep. The room felt so heavy and dense that I couldn't breathe. Everything around the shadow seemed as if the light was taken from it. The shadow's long thin hands hovered over my family. I tried to say stop but my voice was mute. I was in tears because I felt helpless and feared it was going to hurt them.

Suddenly the man from the kitchen grabbed my ankle then a scream broke the silence. I fell to the ground covering my ears from the horrid sound. When I looked around, both the shadow and man were gone. My mom woke up as soon as she heard me drop to the floor. She asked me what was wrong. I didn't know what to say or where to start, so I told her I had a bad dream and tripped over the blanket when I was headed back to bed. She cheered me up and we both went back to sleep.

We had to leave a little early in the morning since a big storm was on its way and we had to make preparations at our house. Betty eventually moved into a new house, which made me feel she was safer than living in that apartment. Still to this day, I could never forget that evil shadow and that man. They both are branded into my mind. I will never be able to shake off the fear they gave me in Betty's apartment.

7

Wind and Rain

Hurricane season arrived in the Rio Grande Valley and everyone was getting prepared for the incoming storm. Buying lumber, emergency supplies, and other necessary items in case of flooding and power outages. My sister Christina and I went to the supply store with our parents while our oldest sister Yoli stayed at the house. We first stopped at the food market to buy canned goods.

Christina and I wandered around the shopping cart, looking at the piñatas hanging from the ceiling and neon signs above the shelves of the store. We ended up walking around the store together to find snacks. When we were walking down the candy aisle, I found a keychain on the floor. It was gold with a half-moon medallion that had words carved into it. I couldn't remember what was written but the words were on the backside of the medallion.

I stood with the keychain in my hands as my mind went blank. My skin began to crawl as I felt a cold breeze pass my shoulder. I turned to look at the end of the aisle and saw an old woman looking at me. I thought it might have been hers but I felt frightened to walk over to her. When our parents got to the candy aisle, Christina suddenly took the keychain from my hands and showed it to them. I looked for the old woman but she was gone. My parents gave the keychain to a worker in case someone came back to look for it. When we got in line to pay for our groceries, a magazine fell off the rack next to me. I reached down to pick it up. As I lifted the magazine, I found the same keychain as before. I felt confused as I thought we gave it to a worker but somehow it ended up with me again.

I put the magazine back in its place and gave the keychain to my mother. She was also a bit confused but didn't make a big deal about it. When my mother turned in the keychain to the cashier, the cashier told us that it belonged to a worker who quit a few days ago. We noticed it was raining outside so we had to rush to our van and try not to get wet. I felt we were being watched as we packed our groceries in the van. I looked around the parking lot then something caught my attention. It was an old woman standing under the canopy of the store looking in our direction. I nudged Christina to look but she was irritated with me for not packing fast enough. The old woman wore an old nightgown and had frizzy hair. She was too far away to see any more details about her.

When we arrived at the wood supply store, the rain had stopped. Trucks were parked in front to be loaded up with lumber as semis brought more supplies to keep up with the demand. Christina and I jumped on the cart pretending we were pirates on a ship till our mom told us to get off because we were being too loud. We passed by the aisles one by one and I remember thinking it was like flipping channels. Every aisle was telling a different story. Some were packed and lit up while others were lonely and dark.

We eventually got to the lumber department of the store and

began to fill the cart with the supplies we needed. It felt like I was in a beehive as many people were loading their carts around the tall stacks of cut lumber. The light in the store flickered for a moment making several people laugh as they joked about not being able to buy anything if the power went out.

My parents were paying at the cash register while Christina and I were clinging on the side of the cart. I turned to the window to see if it was raining but my heart stopped. I saw the same old woman from the previous store standing outside. This time she was closer and I was able to see more details about her. Her gown had a tint of green mixed in brown like a watercolor effect. Her eyes were slightly open with her head tilted to one shoulder. I crouched down hiding behind the wood panels in the cart hoping she wouldn't see me. Christina told me, "what are you doing?" I told her an old woman standing outside the window. She looked and claimed no one was there. When I got up to check for myself, the old woman was gone.

We arrived at our house and began to board up the windows. We also packed emergency bags just in case we had to evacuate. I could hear the echo of hammers, saws, and drills in the neighborhood as everyone was attempting to prevent any damages from happening to their homes. The storm was expected to make landfall later that night as we were hearing the weather on our radio outside by the patio.

After dinner, the afternoon was quiet as my parents were watching the news and my sisters and I were in our rooms drawing or listening to music. When it began to rain, the thunder rumbled in the distance. The wind howled as the storm was approaching and my mother asked if anyone wanted to see the rain from the front porch. I decided to join her and we both watched the rain through the screen door. Everything had a gray hue clouded over it as the rain and wind blew through the trees.

The rain grew heavier by the hour and the lightning began to spread across the night sky. As my mother was closing the main door, I saw the old woman again. She was across the street next to the light post glaring at our house. Once the door was closed, I peeked through the small opening of the window to see if she was still there. I gasped when I saw the old woman standing closer as she was in our front yard under a tree. I closed the curtain and ran to my room to join my sisters.

After an hour or so, the wind roared as the thunder sounded like trees crashing down. A loud thump was heard outside then lights went out. We all huddled in the hallway to protect ourselves in case one of the windows caved in from flying debris. I heard a faint whisper in my ear. I turned around quickly as I didn't recognize their voice. There was a shadow figure at the end of the dark hallway. With every flash of lightning, the shadow got closer to me. I couldn't move no matter how hard I tried. The shadow jumped to the edge of my feet revealing its identity. It was the old woman. She leaned in towards me, opening her mudded eyes. Her jaw was displaced leaving her mouth wide open. Bugs were crawling out and onto her face. It began to smell of rotten meat in her presence.

The old woman stuck out her thin hands reaching for my neck. I lifted my arm to protect myself from her. Suddenly a light appeared behind me causing her to disappear. Christina was staring at me with a concerned face while holding a flashlight in her hands. I'm sure she saw the old woman too but decided to never talk about it. We went to the kitchen where the rest of our family was and sat around the table with candlelights.

Nothing else happened that night. The storm had passed during the early hours of the morning. When we went outside, we noticed one of the trees in our yard had fallen over. If anyone or anything was under it, it would have been deadly. I haven't encountered that old woman again and Christina claims she doesn't recall seeing her that night. Now I'm wary of picking up items wherever I go because this memory lives in the back of my mind.

8

Hush Hush

It was one of the last times we had a family cookout at my grandparent's ranch. We all did the usual routine of either setting up the tables, preparing food or decorating the patio. Us kids had to either help out or stay out of the way.

One of my uncles brought kites for us to play within the new empty lot next door. The strong wind made each of our kites fly high and the lot was spacious enough for us to stay out of each other's way. I remember my sisters and cousins having so much fun that day as we flew kites and played tag in the open space. My grandparent's ranch had many thick trees that made it hard to run through the tight spaces. We also didn't like the spiders that loved to hang around the trees.

We were all sunned out and walked back to our grandparent's

ranch to cool off. I remember my sister Christina calling out to me, pointing to the end of the empty lot. She asked, "Who is that over there?" A person standing alone by the small canal that borders the lot from our grandparent's ranch. They were too far for us to recognize them. We both told our cousins to look but the person was gone. We thought it could have been someone who lived down the street and paid no attention to it since we were very tired.

All of us went inside and basically collapsed all around the house. The big kids obviously took the rooms with the fans and beds while us kids were stuck in the hot living room. The only air that came in was through the front screen door. I still remember the loud clack the door would make as someone opened or closed it.

Since Christina and I were short, we both were able to fall asleep on the couch. It wasn't ideal as its old vintage fabric seemed to suck in all the humidity of the room. Its armrests were cushionless and bare but it was better than sleeping on the concrete floor.

I woke up to the sound of Christina's voice. I thought she was asking me a question or needed something from me. I stood up and looked at her because I couldn't understand what she was saying. After a brief moment, I noticed she was taking in her sleep. Her eyes were closed as she kept speaking in a low voice. I shook her, calling her name but she wouldn't budge. She began to speak in a louder tone so I was able to cipher her words.

"Who are you?
"Christina, it's me, Liz!"
"No, Who is that?"

Once I heard those words, fear hit me. She picked up her hand and pointed towards the direction of the tv. In the corner edge of the tv box, I saw a shadow peeking behind. I thought my sister and cousins were playing a prank. I shook my sister's shoulder telling her to "stop joking around" but her eyes were still closed. I looked around the room while still sitting on the couch to see if anyone else was there with us.

The shadow moved and it stood up in the corner of the room. With each passing second, it grew taller and taller. I could feel the air getting dense as the shadow darkened the room. Christina broke the silence saying "who is it?" I looked at her again and she was still talking in her sleep. I responded, "I don't know." The shadow began to walk towards us. I tried to wake her up but she still wouldn't budge. I leaned over to get in front of her as it got closer.

After I did that, the shadow went back to the same spot as before. It stayed there for a moment and it felt like we had a mini staredown. The shadow began to move around the room. It moved like a snake sliding across the walls at a slow pace. It eventually stopped in front of the bedroom door where my cousins were sleeping. I heard a low growl as it suddenly began to seep under the door and into the other room.

Once the shadow disappeared, I heard a loud thud. My cousins began to scream, waking everyone up. My mom and aunts who were still preparing the food ran to the room. The shelf had fallen over spilling everything out. They tried to figure out how it happened but it was left unsure. Our cousins were still a bit scared after waking up to the loud noise.

I asked Christina, "Who were you talking to? In your dream?" She said she couldn't remember and went outside to play with my cousins. I stayed inside because I still wanted to investigate the shadow. I didn't feel as scared because my mom and aunts were still inside the house with me.

First, I looked into the room where the shelf had fallen. I checked behind the door, under the bed, in the standing closet, then did the same thing to the other rooms in the house. The only room that was left unchecked was by the kitchen. I maneuvered around my mother and aunts as they were preparing the side dishes. The room was empty and quiet though the clanks of pots were still loud enough to hear.

The large window of the room faced the pond while the other faced the side of the front patio. I checked behind the door and under the bunk bed. There was no closet in the room so I didn't have to worry about that. I decided to check the top bunk bed and began to climb. Once I was up there, I stayed for a bit since I never had a chance to do so.

I was playing with a few stuffed animals my cousin had on the top bunk when I saw something in the corner of my eye. It was a woman I did not recognize. She looked like an insane person as she grinned menacingly at me. Her hair was messy, almost burnt, and her clothes looked like she was rolling in the dirt.

She began to giggle, twisting side to side like a child who was too shy to play. I tried to move but my hands were frozen in place. The woman began to climb the ladder of the bunk bed and panic had set in. Once she reached the top, I saw her face more clearly.

She looked gross and sick. Her skin had the same colors of an infected wound with bloodshot eyes. I thought about calling out for my mom but I didn't know how she would react. When the woman put her hand on the bunk as if she was about to hop on, I let out a short gasp. She then lifted her hand and said "Shhh". It sounded like the hissing of a snake.

Thankfully, my mom opened the door telling me it was time for everyone to go outside since the food was ready. The woman had disappeared in an instant. I told my mom what had happened and she blessed the inside of the house as everyone was outside. I stayed with her as she went room by room, blessing it with holy water and prayer.

I felt more at ease and the house did feel a bit lighter inside. The dark wooden walls in the living room didn't seem as heavy as before. We went outside and the afternoon breeze felt refreshing. The party continued and we all ate, danced, and played family games.

The night began to fade in through the canopy of trees. The branches made the sky look like shattered glass. The bright orange from the fire contrasted with the surrounding tones of tree trunks and tall grass. We all sat around the fire eating smores or snacks while talking. Time seemed to pause for a moment.

A loud snap came from the thick trees by the pond. We all turned our heads and took it as a cue to pack up and go home. It must have been past midnight so everyone pitched in to help speed up the cleaning process. Once everything was done, we all left to our separate homes. My grandma packed plates to go and waved us goodbye as we left the ranch.

The following times I visited my grandparent's ranch, I never saw that lady again. The only thing that stayed was the shadow. Who knows if it is still there today.

9

Best Friend

When I was in middle school, Christina invited me to her friend Nora's sleepover. I didn't really know any of her friends but she wanted me to go with her anyway. We packed our things and left for Nora's house. Since our age gap is only about two years, it wasn't hard for me to get along with her friends. It was fun for a while but their loud bubbly selves were too much for me. I was usually a mellowed-out kid so I sat in the living room to catch a break.

That was when I noticed Nora's younger sister. She must have been around six or seven. She looked very sick as her red eyes and nose stood out from her pale face. She sniffled as she approached me with a doll in her hand. The girl asked me my name and why I was there. I told her, "I'm Liz, my sister invited me to join Nora's sleepover. What's your name?" She told me her name was Jacklyn and Nora didn't want her around us.

I proceeded to talk to her for a while as I could tell she was bored and alone. Every now and then she would look to the left or right of me. Her facial expressions would change depending on whether she was looking at me or behind me.

After a few minutes, our sisters walked in with their other friends. Nora yelled at Jacklyn saying, "I don't want you getting near my friends! Go away!" She looked in the corner in the room and Nora yelled again. "What, is it your imaginary friend?" Nora rolled her eyes and stormed out of the living room. We all heard her complain to her mom but her mom told Nora to let Jacklyn play with us.

When she got back, she brought an ouija board. Christina and I looked at each other with concerned faces. Our mom always told us to never play with those things because bad things might happen. I decided to sit out but Christina joined her friends because they pressured her to play. They asked several questions and got bored when nothing happened within a few minutes.

We ended up watching a movie before getting ready to go to bed in the living room. The older kids slept on the couches while the rest of us slept on the floor. Since everyone was still wide awake, we listened to some music on Nora's stereo. I noticed Jacklyn was talking to her doll all alone beside the couch. In the corner of my eye, I saw a shadow duck behind the couch next to her. Nora also noticed Jacklyn and proceeded to nag at her. "Stop being weird. You are going to creep everyone out. No one wants to hear about your stupid friend." Jacklyn began to cry and ran to her room. I felt bad for her but there wasn't anything I could do. We all eventually fell asleep after hearing music and munching on snacks.

I woke up to someone tapping my shoulder. It was Jacklyn and she had a couple of dolls and a blanket in her hand. She sat by my feet and asked if I wanted to play with her dolls. I told her I was okay and that she could stay there if she wanted to. I was going to go back to sleep but she asked me if I saw something earlier. Her question reminded me of the shadow I saw earlier in the room. I replied, "how do you know I saw something?" Jacklyn stated that her "best friend," told her I did. She pointed towards the edge of the couch and said, "Look, he is sitting right there." Those words sent chills to my spine. I was hesitant to look but my curiosity got the best of me. I remember her saying, "doesn't he look nice?" I asked her to describe him because I saw something else. She said he looked like a regular boy who goes to school as she did. He was her height, wore a t-shirt, and blue jeans. I saw something completely different.

It was a small thin looking figure trying to mimic the appearance of a child. It's skin was dry and cracked all over and its clothes were old and worn. The figure's bare feet were covered in mud. It was crouching in the corner looking at Jacklyn with its wide eyes. They were a deep blue color that covered the whites of its eyes. I asked her how she knew it was her friend. She responded that he is the only one who talks to her at home.

I wondered why we saw different things in the room. She saw a boy and I saw something trying to look like one. I asked her if I could take a closer look at her friend. She said yes, so I began to move slowly towards it. The figure looked at me with its wide eyes, watching every movement I made. It began to smell like damp soil when I got close and the air felt dense as if I was trapped in a box trying to breathe. All of a sudden I heard Nora scream, waking everyone up. Everyone in the room started to freak out while Jacklyn and I stayed confused by their reaction. Nora's mom ran in asking what was happening. Nora said she saw something in the room. I could only assume she saw the same thing I did.

We all had to go back home after the incident and that was the first and last time we spent the night at Nora's house. Christina and her friends never mentioned that sleepover ever again. Eventually, they all stopped talking to each other since they went to different middle schools. I still wonder who or what Jacklyn's friend was and if they are still together to this day.

10

Crying Cold

It was around late November when my oldest sister Yoli and I experienced something creepy at our house. I heard something strange outside my window. We have a metal fence in the front yard and when you kick or lean against it, it makes a shaky metallic noise. I was staying up late watching t.v when I heard a thump on the front porch. I opened the curtain thinking something fell down but everything seemed normal. After a few moments, I heard it again but this time it was louder. I turned off the t.v and noticed it was strangely quiet outside. There were no crickets, birds, or dogs barking like they usually do during the night.

I heard wings flapping and then a thump on the metal fence. It must have been a large bird since I was able to hear it from across my room. The loud silence of the neighborhood made it more creepy. I thought, "maybe it's a big owl or a bird?" I had a weird feeling but I ignored it and continued to watch my show until I fell asleep.

The following day before going to school, I found a feather in the kitchen by my door. I thought it was an odd coincidence because of what I heard that night. I blew it off and headed to the bus stop because I was running late. At school, I told my friend about it and she said it could have been a Lechuza. I had no idea what that was so she explained it to me. It's believed that witches who turn into owls try to get you to go outside by making random noises. Once you step out, they either take you or kill you. So in summary, they are shape-shifting witches who could kill or kidnap you. My first impression of the Lechuza was strange but I gave it the benefit of the doubt. There are things out there that we humans will never know.

When I got home, I told Yoli about it since we shared rooms at the time. I had to alter the story a bit since she gets scared easily. She thought it was creepy then asked if I could help her make several canvases for her painting class to change the subject. After dinner, we began to stretch the canvas over the wood frame. Going across one side to the other one by one. When it was around 10 pm, our sister Christina got sick and had to go to the hospital. We stayed behind while everyone else left the house.

Once we finished stretching and stapling the canvases, we started to prime them. It must have been over an hour when we finished all the coats on each of the canvases. We put everything away and sat down to watch a movie while we waited for our family to get back.

Out of nowhere, a loud shrieking came from outside our window. It sounded like a woman distraught and crying desperately. It was an awful thing to hear. We were both scared as we didn't know where it was coming from. I told Yoli, "Maybe it's the neighbors? Maybe something happened to them?" She was too scared to look out the window so I did. I looked around and saw nothing. The crying was still there, loud and haunting as ever.

I went around the house looking through all the windows to see if anyone was in our yard but nothing. The crying was only by our window. We began to hear a scraping noise on the side of the house then a thump. My sister got behind me and said, "What do we do?" We didn't want to worry our parents since they were taking care of Cristina so we just had our phones ready to call for help if we had to.

The crying moved to the porch and it got worse. The closest description of the sound would be similar to a woman crying after losing somebody they truly cared for. The crying sounded like it was literally on the other side of the glass. We both opened the curtain and still, nothing. I was tempted to open the door but I remembered the story my friend had told me. I kept the door closed and looked one last time out the window. Since there was no one to be found, I left.

It lasted for about 30 minutes then there was only silence. No dogs or other animals were making their usual noises in the night. We were surprised that no one in the neighborhood had reported the haunting cries. It made us think that we might have been the only ones able to hear it.

Yoli left all the lights on in the house and we decided to stay in the kitchen until the others came back home. We decided to keep the story to ourselves. It's a memory we will never forget.

11

Carnival by Amigoland

The Amigoland mall used to be an interesting place to visit when I was young. Before it closed down, there were still a few stores open that I remember vividly. There was an arcade that had retro lights and machines all over the place. The last day they were open, I won a small unicorn figurine and decided to keep the only arcade coin I had left. There was also an indoor skating rink, petshop, antique Chinese shop, and a few unique small cafes. The brand businesses like Dillards and JCPenny had relocated to the newly built mall across town. After a year or two, the Amigoland mall was reused as a tech building for the local college. I still refer to it as Amigoland or the Old Mall.

Every November the carnival would come to town and set up across the old mall. It gave that side of town a bit of life as its bright lights shined in the night. The parking lot would be filled with cars as many families went to enjoy their night out. Sometimes the weather would be insanely hot or nice and cold. Regardless of the temperature, it was always packed.

One November day, I went to the carnival with a couple of friends. Some of us had recently got our driver's licenses so we were able to stay out late. We ended up driving separate cars since we all didn't fit in one and visited the shops downtown to waste time.

After a long while of shopping, we all decided to buy food and eat at a park not too far from downtown. Though the sun had already set, the park had enough lights to eat at the picnic tables. When we were done eating, we drove to the carnival.

Since we arrived late, we had to park far into the Old Mall lot. The small canal behind the building always weirded me out but that area was the only space left. We got off and walked a good distance to the carnival. There were two streets side by side that we had to cross to get to the carnival. As we crossed the first street and made it to the concrete in between, I felt as if we were being watched. Sure, there were other people around us, but I couldn't shake off the strange feeling.

Once we crossed the second street, I was able to take my mind off it and enjoy the night with my friends. I mostly played games as my friends got on all the rides several times over. I was able to win a few prizes for my friends and family. Most of them were small but I was able to win a couple of medium-sized ones.

The cool air began to sink in. We stayed a bit longer until there were hardly any people left. Some of us got hungry again so we were deciding on what to do. Half of the group left to go eat at Denny's while the others left to eat at Whataburger. My close friend and I weren't really hungry so we decided to go home.

As we were walking to our cars, it began to fog. The tall grass beside the Old Mall made the atmosphere more ominous. The noise of the carnival grew faint as we continued to walk to our cars. Our steps sounded like crunching snow in the loose gravel. The outdated yellow street lights looked like glowing spheres in the fog. My extroverted friends laughed and jumped, making all the noise in the world. I always enjoyed their carefree attitude. It was refreshing to be in their company. Once we got to our cars, we all went our separate ways.

My close friend didn't want to go home yet so we decided to walk around the old mall. We were worried a bit about the night security guard but figured he was busy monitoring the main parking lot. We walked around the front, seeing cars leave as the fog grew thicker. By the time we arrived at the opposite side of the building, the fog was so dense that we couldn't see a few yards in front of us. This was when we decided to head back to my car and go home.

Behind the old mall was dark as only a couple of lights had worked. The fog made every sound coming from the small canal eerier. I heard a few splashes and rustling in the tall grass but tried not to think much of it. When we were about halfway from our walk back, he got a phone call from his mother. He asked me to wait for him as he stepped away for a moment to talk to her.

I sat down on the curb to give him some space and messaged our other friends to see if they were still out or not. Only two of them were still at Denny's while the rest had already gone home. As I was sitting, I heard a noise coming from the grass by the canal. I stood up and looked in that direction.

There was a silhouette of a person standing in the grass. The fog was dense so I wasn't able to see who it was. Thinking it could be a weirdo or creeper, I began to walk towards my friend. I noticed the silhouette seemed to walk with me within the fog. When I walked it walked and when I stopped it stopped. I leaned right to left and it was still mimicking my movements. Shivers ran down my spine. I thought I was going crazy. I didn't want to make a scene so I continued to walk towards my friend while still keeping an eye on the silhouette. Again, it weirdly followed my movements. Suddenly I tripped and fell on the sidewalk. I noticed my shoes were untied and laughed at myself because I felt so dumb.

The shadow was gone but somehow it made me feel more uneasy. I saw my friend standing under the archway on the far end of the building. He was still on the phone and I could tell it was something serious just by his posture. I began to pick myself up from the ground. This was when I heard footsteps approaching me on the sidewalk. I expected it to be the security guard so I waited to see if it was him or not. I could see a figure in the fog slowly approaching. It moved awkwardly in the darkness between the empty spaces of the light, almost like it wanted to crawl on the floor. I got a bad feeling just by looking at it.

I got up from the floor and walked backward to keep my eyes on it. I was passing one of the loading docks behind the building. The gaping space made me feel like I was out in the open. The bright lights from the storage doors exaggerated the haze of the fog. The figure began to run towards me. My heart dropped and I froze for a split second until I mustered the courage to run.

As I was turning around to run, a person standing behind me, I stopped in place trying to comprehend what was happening. The person looked like a decomposing corpse as their skin looked like chipped wall paint full of mold and rot. Its eyes were empty lifeless sockets and there were missing pieces of flesh on the left side of its face. Though this sight was terrifying, I couldn't make a sound. The only thing I was able to do was stare at it.

The person was close enough for me to hear their breathing. The raspiness of their breath sounded like a hiss. I moved slowly against the wall trying to get away but I stumbled and fell down again. When I got up, the person and figure in the fog had disappeared. I felt a hand on my shoulder and I flinched slightly. It turned out to be my friend and he asked me why I was so startled. I ended up telling him I was tired after a long day of being out.

Once we got in my car, I looked at the surrounding fog hoping I wouldn't see those things again. I started to drive up the road passing the train tracks. I felt my arms getting cold. I looked at the empty field by the railroad crossing and saw the two figures standing there. Once I left that area, I didn't see anything else on the drive back to my house.

12

The Old Fort Morgue

Even though I have seen things I cannot explain, I was still not a believer of the local legends in our city. We have the Llorona, the ghosts of Fort Brown, the haunted Colonial Hotel, and ghost cows of 511. Yes, you read that right. We have ghost cows that appear out of nowhere late at night causing accidents.

The community college and University in Brownsville, Texas are stationed where Fort Brown used to be. Fort Brown was a military base during the Mexican-American War around the mid to late 1840s. One of the old buildings still standing on campus ground is the Old Fort Morgue which housed thousands of bodies during the outbreak of Yellow Fever. People began to believe that the spirits of cavalry soldiers, victims of the outbreak, and casualties of past battles walk among campus grounds.

Every Halloween the campus would have ghost tours at night for people who were looking for a fright. The tour guides would explain the history and backgrounds of Fort Brown while leading people to and around the Old Fort buildings. I remember the tour guide telling us that many of the buried bodies near the morgue had resurfaced after a major flood. The bodies had been relocated after the incident. It was a fun experience to explore and learn about the history of our city.

In my early college years, I went to the community college where most of the Old Fort buildings reside. I had to take night classes since those were the only ones available at the time. I didn't mind it but it was creepy walking alone across campus since there weren't that many people around. The paths connecting the buildings seemed abandoned while the mesquite trees mimicked shadows in the dark. Though you try not to think about the ghost stories of the Old Fort, you couldn't help but do so as you walk past the buildings.

One night, my professor canceled class at the last minute, making me wait for my next class. I decided to walk around instead of driving back and forth from campus to my house. I was walking to the Olivera Library across campus. I could see the Old morgue from the path and its small light on top of its door made it seem menacing.

I heard footsteps coming from behind me. Naturally, I turned around to see if anyone was there but the path was empty. I continued to walk towards the library. Everything was fine as I enjoyed the silence and cool breeze. I decided to check out the Old Morgue and the old hospital building since I love spooky things.

The bricks holding the structure spoke for themselves. The erosion of the elements showed its history and endurance over the years. I traced the bricks as I walked around the building peering in the windows and wondering about the lives of the people who worked or died there.

I ended up in the mini rose garden next to where the old hospital used to be. I sat down and listened to the surrounding silence. A tapping noise came from the patio of the building. I walked over to investigate what caused it. As I got to where I believe it came from, I saw something move in the corner of my eye. The hair in the back of my neck rose. I called out saying hello but I got no response.

I decided it was time to head back to the North Hall where my next class was at. When I was walking back, I saw a woman sitting on the path next to the light post. She was crouched down holding her knees within her arms. The woman's clothes were covered with dirt and her hair was messy. She had no backpack or bags on her so I thought she might have been a homeless person. The campus is open so anyone could basically wander around.

No one else was on the path but us. When I got close to her, she shot up to stand. The casting of the light covered the top half of her face and chest. I waved hello, acknowledging her presence but she stood in silence. When I was in front of her, I heard her mumble something. I stopped to see if she was trying to ask me a question. The woman began to walk towards me then I heard the sound of a bike coming from behind. A guy shouted, "Excuse me!" from his bike as I moved over to let him pass. When I turned back to the woman, she was gone.

I made it to my second class and the three-hour lecture began. Class ended at 10 pm and everyone practically bolted out of the classroom. I parked on the South Hall lot by the canal so I had to walk through the building to get to my car. I had an old Hyundai accent which was basically a mini car but it got me to where I needed to go.

Like the paranoid person that I am, I always check under my car and in the back seat before I enter to make sure no creeper is around. Everything was clear and I got in my car to go home. As I got to the light stop by the gym, I saw the woman again. She was standing on the sidewalk alone. I was driving for about a minute then the radio turned on. It was usual since the car was old and had a tendency to go haywire. I turned it off and continued driving.

I was passing the park next to the university when I heard a tapping noise on the back window. I looked into the rearview mirror and saw the woman sitting in the backseat. I stopped the car and looked again but the woman disappeared. Luckily, there were no people around because they would have thought I was crazy for stopping in the middle of the road. I blamed my lack of sleep and tried to brush it off. Once I got to my house, I took a shower and went to bed. I woke up to the sound of tapping on my bedroom window. I stood for a moment thinking whether or not to open the curtain and look outside. I opened the curtain only to find a branch brushing against the window by the wind. I laughed it off and went back to sleep.

The following week, I had my night classes again. Everything was normal for the rest of the night until my last class was over. I was walking back to my car across South Hall ready to go home. As I was walking, I heard footsteps behind me. I turned around but no one was there. I waited for a moment to check my surroundings then headed back to my car. My keys fell out of my hand and onto the floor. As I reached down to pick them up I saw a pair of feet in front of me. I immediately got back up but no one was there. This creeped me out and I wanted to leave as soon as possible.

I was sitting in the driver's seat when I heard a noise behind me. In the rearview mirror, I saw the woman from before standing outside the car. Suddenly she began to walk towards the passenger seat window. Her face was covered by her shadow as the parking lot light was above us. She was peering in the car as she walked forward while tapping the glass with her fingers. I expected her to stop at the passenger window but she continued to walk forward. Once she was in the blind spot between the front and side window, she disappeared. I was confused. I thought, where did she go? I decided to look around and under my car just in case before I left.

I started to drive off and turned on the radio to clear my mind. When I went over the speed bumps, the radio turned off. In that silence, I heard someone giggle inside the car. I looked to my left and saw the woman sitting in the passenger seat. I stopped the car and got out. I expected the passenger door to open but nothing happened. I looked inside and there was no one to be found. Cars were approaching so I got back in my car and continued to drive home.

Later that night before I went to bed, I tried to look up some information on the woman I saw. I wanted to know if other people on campus had a similar experience to mine. Nothing showed up other than the basic information on the hauntings of the Old Fort Brown. I never saw that woman again.

13

Fire

I decided to hang out with my friends one late afternoon. It was the weekend and we all planned to eat dinner at the event center in town. We bought some food, snacks, and ate at the tables by the river. When we were done eating, we decided to drive around town doing random things. One of my friends suggested dumpster diving behind some craft and makeup stores. They found some items that were still in good shape and placed them in the trunk. My friends got bored and suggested that we drive through the old cemetery. We thought nothing of it and went over instantly.

The streets leading toward the cemetery appeared more narrow in the night. We almost got lost but thankfully google maps saved us. We drove slowly through the cemetery. There was only one way in and out so there was no backing out once we went through the gate. My friends claimed they saw a woman walking and vanishing just outside the wall that borders the cemetery. We took several pictures but they all came out terrible due to poor lighting. The only light came from the streetlamps outside the cemetery. It made it feel more dark and secluded from downtown. Nothing happened so we continued to drive around the city till midnight. We all messaged each other after arriving home and went to sleep.

I was taking classes out of town and had to drive an hour each day to arrive at the art building. One class ended at 8 pm so I'd usually be home by 9 pm. This was when the sun would set around 7 and I basically had to drive in the night.

For several days, I kept seeing a girl in the restroom though I was completely alone. Each day I got to see more detail of her. The first day, she was standing outside the stall. I could see her converse shoes from my side of the door. I went over to wash my hands expecting someone to exit but no one did. All the stalls were open and it was empty. The second day, I went to the restroom and all the stalls were open so I knew I was the only one in there. Again, as I went over to wash my hands, I saw her standing in the stall from the restroom mirror. The stall was open though it looked like she was trying to hide. I turned around but she was gone.

This kept happening for two more days. I waited in the restroom for a brief moment. I felt the spirit was trying to tell me something so I began to talk to it. I remember saying, "If you want to tell me something I'm here to listen." No one was there but I wanted the spirit to know I was willing to hear it out.

One of my classes was canceled at the last minute. Since I didn't want to drive back home and come back for my noon class, I decided to stay in the lab and work on my designs. The next class that used the lab wouldn't be there for a few hours so I had enough time to catch up on my work.

Everything was pretty chill since it was just me in the lab. I was listening to music and working on assignments but then the lights turned off. If no one is using the lab for an hour, the lights turn off automatically to save power. I had forgotten about this and it startled me when it happened. The only light in the room came from my computer and the tiny window beside the door. The darkness all around the room gave me an eerie feeling. I tried stomping so that the sensor could hear that I'm in the room but it wouldn't budge.

I was sitting in the last row and had to walk over to the light switch in the front. As I was walking, I saw someone crouching down in the second row. I jumped back holding my breath as it caught me off guard. The person also jumped by my reaction. I leaned in for a split moment to see if it was another student but they moved away so that I couldn't get a closer look. At this moment, I noticed something was off about the person's appearance. It looked as if they had fallen into thick matted tar, almost disappearing into the darkness of the room.

This was when I realized that it was an apparition and not a human being. I remember the reptile-like eyes it had when they stared at me in the dark. Their presence felt evil like it wanted to cause harm if I looked away. I kept staring at the apparition as I walked toward the light switch. It continued to move back, trying to hide from my view behind one of the rolling chairs. When I managed to turn on the light, the apparition was gone. I looked all around the classroom, checking row by row, but no one was there.

I thought stress was getting to me, making me see things that aren't there. I messaged my mom and Yoli telling them what happened. I tried to continue to work on my assignment but the lights switched off again. I immediately jumped up and looked towards the same spot hoping not to see that thing again. The sensor heard my chair rolling back and the lights turned back on. I was expecting them to turn off after another hour but not even 5 minutes had passed when they switched off in the room. I packed my stuff and left. I ate my late lunch in the car while waiting for my last class. I was still talking with my mom and sister while trying to figure out what I saw.

In my last class, we were discussing the senior exhibit art show. We were deciding on the theme, logo, and colors of the event. After a few minutes, the fire alarm rang. We waited a moment thinking it was a false alarm but there was smoke in the hallway. Everyone got their things and went outside. The fire engines came and went into the building. I overheard the professors mentioning a small fire broke out in the woodshop class. The fire only took a few moments to put out. All of us were waiting outside as the large fans blew the smoke out of the building. The class continued as usual when it was clear.

The sun had already set and I was ready to head home after class. I was driving on the highway for a couple of minutes till I felt chills roll down my spine. When I looked in the rearview mirror, I saw a silhouette of someone sitting in the back seat. The shadow was transparent as I could see the streetlights through it as I drove. At this point, I knew it was a spirit and not an actual human being. I thought of what to do. Should I park on the side of the road or do something else? I remembered that when you visit haunted places, you must tell the spirits or entities to not follow you home. I was keeping my eye on the road as I said, "I do not allow you to follow me. You need to leave". I repeated this several times before looking back into the rearview mirror. It was gone and I felt more at ease while I was driving.

As I got to the front of my house, I said it once more just to be extra safe. I put away all my stuff, took a shower, and went to bed. After that night, I never saw that girl or entity again. I wanted to talk to the front desk to see if they caught anything on camera since all the labs have them but didn't want to be labeled as crazy. I also didn't want to raise any flags since it was the same day as the fire so I kept it to myself. I still wonder about it though, and I could only imagine the camera capturing my reaction and that thing in the room.

Notes

I believe everyone may have ability to interact with spirits or entities. Some of us are unaware of our capabilities as we never attempted to focus our energy on them. I hope the reader will ask themselves questions after reading these stories. Why did I get a certain feeling about a place or person? Why am I seeing or hearing things others cannot?

I wanted to share my experiences and give a better understanding to those who may also be going through the same thing. People may doubt or question your experiences but the only thing that matters is your own thoughts and emotions. I believe everyone is connected to the earth and its energy. The only thing we must do is feel and listen.

The glossary is a starting point for the reader to gain more knowledge of their inner psyche if they wish to do so. This is a small list of psychic abilities people most identify with though there are many others out there. Explore wisely.

Glossary

Clairaudience

The ability to hear things others cannot

Hearing ringing or high-pitched sounds

Hearing messages in music or other audio sources

You are overwhelmed by intense noise

Hearing voices calling your name when you are alone

Talking to yourself randomly

Claircognizance

The ability of intuition or inner knowing

You experience deja-vu frequently

You often guess correctly based on instinct or gut feelings

You are always lost in thought

Find solutions to problems without prior knowledge

Your love to learn and absorb tons of information

Clairalient

The ability to smell things others cannot

You are able to smell diseases or illness in people or animals

Intense smells cause headaches or dizziness

You could smell feelings or energies of others

Smelling the scent of those who have passed

Odors or scents appear randomly without cause

Clairsentience

The ability to feel emotions from another's perspective

You sense energies in people, places, or things

Highly sensitive to your surroundings and environment

You are very empathetic and cry easily

You are able to feel subtle changes in temperature

Large crowds are overwhelming to you

Clairvoyance

The ability to see things beyond the visible in our world

Vivid imagery of past events appear in your mind

You see shadows or beings others cannot

You often see orbs, colors, or lights appear in front of you

You experience premonitions on events, people, or things

You see energies of people, animals, or objects around you

Healer

The ability feel the pain of others

People approach you when they feel the need to open up

You have a constant feeling to help others

You help others feel resolve in their lives

You have a strong sense of compassion to heal and help people

You feel drained after social events with large crowds

Disclaimer

To maintain the anonymity of the individuals involved, I have changed some details. These are my memories, from my perspective, and I have tried to represent events as faithfully as possible. Some sample scenarios in this book are fictitious. Any similarity to actual persons, living or dead, is coincidental.

This book does not replace the advice of a medical professional. Consult your physician, psychologist, or health professional before making any changes to your regular health plan.

www.ingramcontent.com/pod-product-compliance
Lightning Source LLC
Chambersburg PA
CBHW021935170626
46807CB00007B/3125